Country Companions

The Picnic

Written by Karen King

Illustrations by Rosemary Sharman

By courtesy of Hallmark Cards UK

MADCAP

'Anyone home?' called Sam Rabbit as he stepped into Ed Hedgehog's kitchen.

'In here!' Ed called. He'd been snoozing in his favourite armchair while Tom was out shopping.

Ed sat up and yawned as Sam came into the lounge.

'Morning, Ed,' said Sam. 'I've just popped in to see if you and Tom would like to join us on a picnic this afternoon.'

'Oh, yes, we'd love to!' said Ed. 'I'll bring some peanut butter sandwiches and mashed potatoes and ice cream and fizzy pop ...'

Ed was so busy planning all the food he was going to take on the picnic that he hardly listened to Sam.

'Right, see you both there at two o'clock then,' said Sam as he left.

Ed started to prepare the picnic food straight away.

Ed had made a huge pile of peanut butter sandwiches when Tom returned with the shopping.

'Goodness, you must be hungry!' said Tom. 'That's a lot of sandwiches, even for you!'

'They're for the picnic,' said Ed. He told Tom that Sam had invited them to a picnic that afternoon.

'It's a good job I went shopping then,' said Tom, taking a loaf, some crisps, ham, cheese and lemonade out of his shopping bag.

Ed and Tom packed a picnic hamper full of food. Well, almost full – Ed couldn't resist eating some of it.

'We'd better get a move on,' said Ed, looking at the clock. 'The picnic starts at two o'clock.'

'We'd have been ready a bit sooner if you hadn't kept tucking into the food!' Tom reminded him, laughing.

Ed picked up the picnic hamper and off they went.

'Where is the picnic?' asked Tom.

Ed clapped his hand to his forehead. 'Oh dear, I can't remember where Sam said they were going!' he said.

So they decided to try the meadow first. It was quite a long walk and Ed got a bit hungry on the way, so he had a little snack from the picnic basket.

When they arrived at the meadow there was no sign of Sam and the other Country Companions.

'Perhaps they're picnicking in the top field,' suggested Tom. So they walked to the top field. Ed got a bit hungry on the way so he had another little snack.

When they arrived at the top field all they found were a couple of cows grazing.

'I wish you could remember where Sam was having the picnic,' sighed Tom. 'All this walking around is making me tired.'

'Me too,' said Ed.

They both sat down for a rest. Ed had another little snack and tried to remember what Sam had told him about the picnic.

'I think, perhaps, they were picnicking by the river,' Ed said.

So the two friends set off for the river.

But Sam and the other Country Companions weren't there either.

'Oh dear, I'm too tired to walk any further,' gasped Ed.

'So am I,' said Tom. 'And I'm hungry. Let's have the picnic here, by ourselves.'

Just then, they heard someone calling them.

'Hey, Ed! Tom! Over here!'

Tom stood up and looked around. Sam and Edwina were standing by the hedge around the meadow, waving to them.

'Where have you been? We've been waiting for you!' shouted Sam.

Ed and Tom were pleased to see their friends. They hurried over to join the picnic.

'I'm starving!' said Tom, opening the picnic hamper. But all he found inside were a few crumbs – Ed had eaten all the food!

Ed felt awful. 'I'm sorry. I didn't mean to eat it all,' he apologised. 'I only had a couple of snacks.'

Luckily, the other Country Companions had lots of food and shared it with Ed and Tom.

They were all tucking into the picnic when Max Mole popped up to join them. 'Is there any food left?' he asked.

'Plenty,' said Edwina. 'Come and join in.'

It was a lovely, lazy afternoon.

'We must do this again soon,' said Tom.

Everyone agreed. 'And next time I won't eat all our food,' promised Ed.

Later, Ed treated Tom to tea at Olivia's café, to make up for eating the picnic food.

'Goodness, Ed, I can't eat all that!' Tom gasped when Ed brought a plate piled high with sandwiches over to the table. 'One sandwich is enough for me!'

'That's okay. I'll eat the rest,' said Ed. 'I'm feeling a bit hungry!'

'Oh, Ed!' laughed Tom.

Other titles in this series

The Birthday Surprise (read and colour)
The Lost Wellingtons
The Photo Competition
The Summer Fayre

The Summer Fayre and **The Lost Wellingtons**
are also available as book and tape and as an audio tape
from MCI Children's Audio

First published in Great Britain by Madcap Books, André Deutsch Ltd, 76 Dean Street, London, W1V 5HA
André Deutsch is a subsidiary of VCI plc
www.vci.co.uk

Text and illustrations copyright © 1998 Madcap Books
Country Companions™ © Hallmark Cards UK

A catalogue record for this title is available from the British Library

ISBN 0 233 99224 3

Printed in the UK